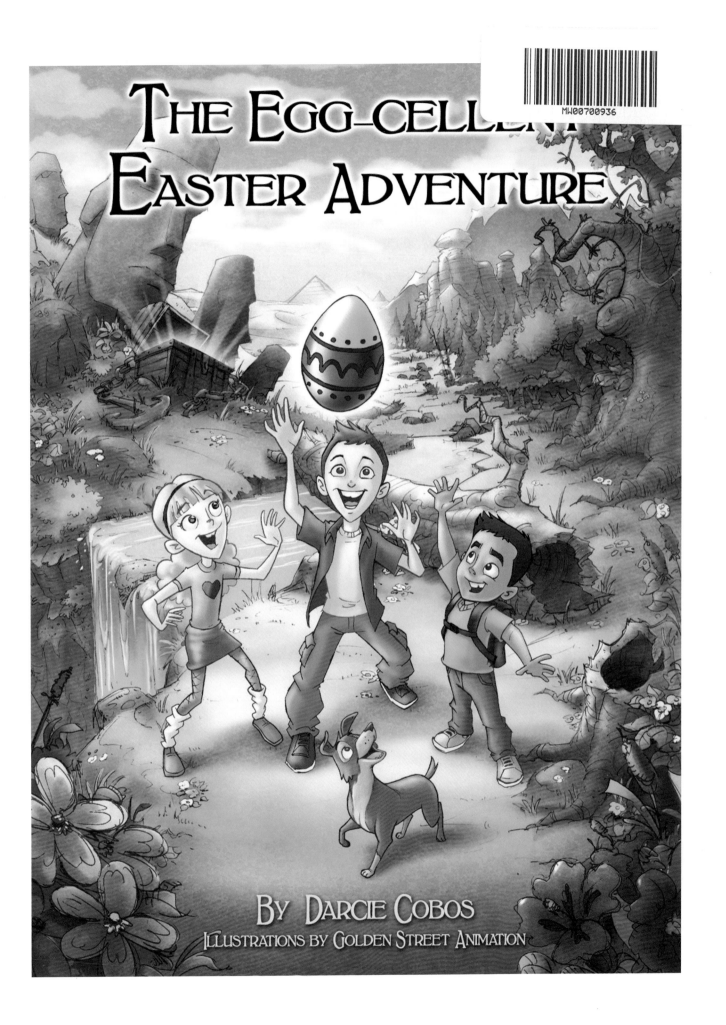

The Egg-cellent Easter Adventure

By Darcie Cobos

Illustrations by Golden Street Animation

THE EGG-CELLENT EASTER ADVENTURE

Copyright © 2012 by Darcie Cobos
Illustrations Copyright © 2012 by Darcie Cobos
No part of this book may be reproduced or transmitted in any form or by any means,
electronic or mechanical, including photocopying, recording or by any information
storage and retrieval system, without permission in writing from the copyright owner.
Published by Carpenter's Son Publishing, Franklin, Tennessee
Published in association with Larry Carpenter of Christian Book Services, LLC
www.christianbookservices.com
Illustrated by Golden Street Animation Productions
www.goldenstreetanimation.com
Cover and Interior Layout Design by Debbie Manning Sheppard
Edited by Lorraine Bossé-Smith and Virginia Bowen
The New International Reader's Version® (NIrV, 1996) is a new Bible version developed
to enable early readers to understand God's message. Begun in 1992 and co-sponsored
by International Bible Society and Zondervan Publishing House,
a simplification of the New International Version (NIV).

Printed in the United States of America
978-09883043-8-3
All rights reserved.

For information regarding Egglo Easter Eggs,
Egglo Treasures bible verse scrolls and glowing
trinkets, curriculums, resources, downloads,
or to order additional books, please visit:
www.eggloentertainment.com

Egglo

*See the light of Jesus
clearly in the dark!*

DEDICATION

First and foremost, I want to thank the Lord for calling
me to this project, inspiring the idea, equipping me
through the journey, and so much more. I pray that
this work is a faithful interpretation of His will.
To Him, belongs the honor and praise.

I dedicate this book to my sons, Trent and Grant, who
are a blessing to me and the lights of my life. Always
remember to let your light shine.

I wish to extend my deepest gratitude to my family
and friends who encouraged and helped me. A
heart-felt thank you to the new friends I made
along the way, and to Virginia Bowen for her help.

A special note of appreciation to
Scott Petersen and the talented artists at
Golden Street Animation
for providing the illustrations.
You can learn more about Golden Street at:
www.goldenstreetanimation.com

It was the Saturday before Easter, Holy Saturday some call it. The family was together and preparing for Easter Sunday. Hardy, Anastasia, and their cousin, Pascal, played together, along with their dog, Zeke. Mom was busy in the kitchen, and Pascal's mom and dad were feeding his baby sister. The kids teamed up to wrestle Dad. Then they played a rousing game of chase the dog, jump over the couch, and bounce off Dad, who let out a funny, "Oomph" with each kid's landing.

"Settle down," Mom insisted. "But we're bored!" complained Hardy. Pascal piped up, "Can we do the Easter egg hunt now?" Mom took a moment to explain, "Patience, Pascal. We are going to a very special Easter egg hunt. It's at night! Can you guess what we will be looking for?" Pascal silently shook his head. "We're going to hunt for eggs that glow in the dark!" Mom announced. Pascal's eyes widened, "Really? That's so cool!"

Mom continued, "Tonight is a program about the meaning of Easter, and God's sacrifice to show His love for us. Afterward, we'll go out onto the lawn with our flashlights to hunt for glowing eggs. The light of the Easter eggs reminds us that Jesus called himself the light of the world. God calls His children to be light to the world, too. You will see how even the smallest light shines through the darkness."

Mom wanted to tell the kids more about Jesus and what they would do at the program that evening, but they weren't paying attention. All the kids could think about was the glow-in-the-dark Easter egg hunt. They were so excited. Over and over they asked, "Is it time yet?" Mom sighed and looked down at Zeke, licking up spilled cupcake batter. To keep the kids busy, Mom sent them up to the attic to find an old board game. The kids scurried off. With one last *SLURP* of batter, Zeke darted after them.

Hardy wanted to be the first one to the attic. Pascal reached the hallway first and grabbed the rope to pull down the attic stairs. Hardy snatched the rope away and ordered, "Wait down here. I'll go up first and check it out." Pascal snapped back, "You're not the boss of me. You're always telling me what to do." Ignoring Hardy, Pascal started up the stairs, but Hardy nearly knocked Pascal down to be first up the steps. "You always have to be first!" Pascal huffed.

Anastasia looked up at the dark attic and whimpered, "I'm scared of the dark." Hardy complained, "You're afraid of everything, Anastasia. But I'll turn the light on." "Call me Ana!" she demanded, then dashed up the stairs. Zeke bounded after her.

At the top of the stairs, they all sighed, "Ooooh!" at the sight of the toys, games, and treasures before them. Pascal headed for a stack of games that was about to fall over. "Wait, let me help you," Ana called out. Pascal didn't listen and grabbed one of the boxes. The whole pile fell over with a *CRASH*, spilling game pieces across the floor. "Look at the mess you made! Why don't you ever listen, Pascal?" grumbled Ana. "I just wanted a game," Pascal pouted.

Startled by the noise, a little mouse ran to hide. Zeke scurried across the floor, chasing the mouse toward some boxes. Zeke scrambled to stop, but crashed into the pile. A little treasure chest flew into the air and something colorful and luminous popped out. Zeke snatched the glowing thing, bounded over to the kids, and plopped it on the floor. The kids all gasped. "What is it?" whispered Pascal.

It was an Easter egg. A ***glowing*** Easter egg!

Ana reached for the egg, but Hardy beat her to it. Pascal took it away from Hardy. "Gimme!" each of the kids shouted, trying to see it first. They grabbed and swatted at each other and the egg, but it rolled away. Everyone dove for it, and all three kids touched the egg at the same time. Suddenly, the egg glowed brighter! And brighter! And brighter! It started shaking and spinning. The kids looked at each other in disbelief. Then, mysteriously it opened, shining even brighter. Two scrolls appeared before their eyes. The scrolls opened one after the other for them to read. Hardy read the first one out loud:

Do nothing out of selfishness, but in humility value others above yourself.

PHILIPPIANS 2:3

"It's a Bible verse," said Ana, knowingly. "But what does it mean?" Pascal asked. Hardy knew the answer, but didn't want to admit it. Ana eyed Hardy and said, "It means we should be humble, and love others more than we love ourselves. Jesus lived that way. He served others." "But what does it mean right now?" asked Pascal. "Maybe the other scroll will tell us," Hardy quickly answered to change the subject.

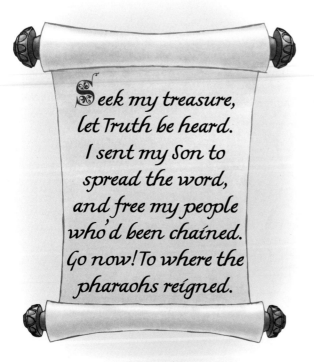

Seek my treasure, let Truth be heard. I sent my Son to spread the word, and free my people who'd been chained. Go now! To where the pharaohs reigned.

Baffled, Hardy, Ana, and Pascal all stared at each other. Ana piped up, "I think it's a riddle." "Maybe it's like a treasure hunt!" Pascal added, excitedly. "I think 'my Son' must be Jesus, but what does 'the word' mean? " Ana wondered. Hardy thought out loud, "Well, Moses freed the Israelite slaves from the Pharaoh who ruled Egypt."

At the word "Egypt," the egg started to glow and glow, brighter and brighter, until it overtook the entire attic. Hardy, Ana, Pascal, and even Zeke, were blinded by a powerful white light, and squeezed their eyes shut.

Suddenly, the light was gone. Blinking until they could see again, they slowly opened their eyes. They weren't in the attic anymore...

HEE HAW! A donkey surprised them. Confused, Pascal asked, "Where are we?" Looking around, they saw pyramids! Real, live, genuine pyramids! Ana gasped, "You guys, I think we're in Egypt! How did *that* happen?" *HEE HAW!* The donkey bellowed again, glancing back at them. "I think the donkey wants us to follow him," guessed Pascal, walking off. "Wait, Pascal. What are you going to do—just follow a donkey through the desert? I'm the oldest. I'm in charge. You need to listen to me," Hardy insisted. Pascal ignored him, and kept walking. Ana shrugged, "I'm afraid we'll get lost. At least the donkey seems to know where he's going," and Ana followed after them. Hardy went along grumbling and complaining.

The donkey stopped in front of a pyramid. Suddenly, the kids began sinking! Down they fell through the sand, sliding down a ramp, and landing with a *THUMP* on the ground below. "Your foot's in my face!" grumped Ana. "Your elbow's in my ear!" grumbled Pascal. "Aarf!" Zeke yelped at Hardy, who was sitting on his tail. They had fallen into some kind of chamber below the pyramids. The donkey peered down from above, and with a snickering *HEE HAW*, disappeared.

Ana cried, "Where are we now? It's spooky down here." Pascal was already exploring, looking at strange drawings on the walls. Hardy said, "We read about these in school. They're Egyptian hiero...hiero glyphics." Looking closer, Pascal was curious, "Huh, that's interesting. That picture looks like Moses. And are those some of the ten plagues?" Ana pointed to the wall, "I think this one's a map! And isn't this the same Easter egg from the attic?" Puzzled, Hardy said, "I wonder if we're supposed to search for another one of those glowing eggs?"

Hardy glanced at the map and declared, "I know what to do. Follow me this way." Ana figured out the map led the other way. She whispered to Pascal to copy the map on some paper from her pocket. Then she tried to talk to Hardy, but he wouldn't listen. Stomping his foot, Hardy insisted, "I'm the oldest. I'm in charge." Grabbing a torch from the wall, he marched off in the wrong direction. Hardy led them down several dark halls, where it was too dark to see. Ana cried, "I'm scared and we're lost." Hardy grunted at her, "No we're not. I know where I'm going."

When they hit a dead end, Hardy finally realized he *didn't* know where he was going, and he didn't know what to do. Now Hardy was upset. Ana gently pointed out, "Remember the Bible verse from the Easter egg? It was about being humble and putting others before ourselves. Have you been treating people the way Jesus did?" Hardy had to admit he had been bossing them around and not listening to what they had to say. Worst of all, wanting to do things his way had gotten them into trouble. Hardy swallowed his pride, and told Ana and Pascal he was sorry.

They forgave Hardy and turned to go back. But when Ana asked Pascal for the copy of the map. Pascal answered, "I didn't do it. I didn't think we'd need it." Ana complained, "Pascal, why don't you listen?" Suddenly, Hardy had an idea, "I see light up ahead; let's just follow where it leads." Together, they followed the torches in the right direction. Up ramps, down ramps, around corners, and down halls they went. "Where did all these lit torches come from anyway?" wondered Pascal. "I dunno, but they are lighting our way," Hardy pointed out.

After a while, they came to another dead end! Ana was sure they had gone the right way. When they stopped to think, Pascal started fidgeting with the carvings on the wall. Hardy warned him, "Stop, Pascal. It could be dangerous." But Pascal didn't listen,

and pushed against a stone sticking out of the wall. A secret door opened. "See," Pascal smiled proudly. "Look at that! What do you think is in there?" asked Hardy. Ana was afraid to go in. Before, Hardy would have ignored her feelings, but now he thought about how he could help her. Hardy bravely stepped inside to show her there was nothing to fear. Down the stairs they went into to a dark, dank room, but with a glowing light coming from another door. Hardy and Pascal pushed the big stone door open. In the room, they discovered another luminous treasure chest, like the one in the attic.

Hardy started to rush forward in excitement, but caught himself. He thought about being humble, and instead waited for the others. Together, they opened the treasure chest, and sure enough, inside was another glowing Easter egg. But it was shut! They looked at each other, unsure what to do. Finally, Pascal realized the other Easter egg in the attic opened when they all had their hands on it together. This time, Hardy went first to encourage them, and put his hand on the egg. Ana and Pascal were a little afraid, and hesitated. Pascal took a deep breath, and then reached out his hand. Ana had to make her hand stop shaking before she finally touched the egg. Instantly, the egg glowed very brightly and began to open. And, just like before, it had two scrolls. The first scroll once again had a Bible verse. Hardy read it for them.

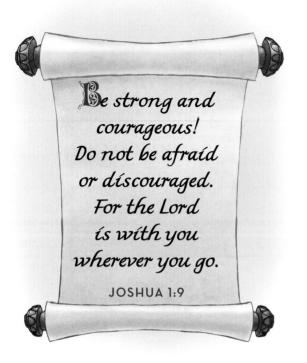

Be strong and courageous! Do not be afraid or discouraged. For the Lord is with you wherever you go.

JOSHUA 1:9

I wonder what that means?" asked Ana. Hardy thought for a minute and then said, "It's what God told Joshua when he led the Israelites into the Promised Land and the Battle of Jericho." He continued, "God promises us that when we're afraid, or we don't know what to do, He will always be there to encourage and help us. We just have to trust God, and pray to Him." Pascal asked, "What's the other scroll say?"

Now to the shore, and on below where treasures sink, and then you'll know The next to visit is a site where strange things dwell with little light.

An idea came to Pascal, "Guys, I think we're on a treasure hunt! I wonder what the treasure will be?" Ana interrupted, "Yeah, but we seem to be hunting for Easter eggs." Hardy speculated, "Hmm, Easter eggs that lead to treasure. I'm not sure what to make of it." Ana chimed in, "If that first riddle was a clue to where we are now, this one must be a clue to where we're going next." Pascal thought, "Well, 'the shore' probably means the ocean." With that, the Easter egg glowed brightly again, and they weren't in Egypt anymore...

The kids found themselves near a beach. Big strange statues of faces stood all around. Hardy spoke first, "I know this place! It's called Easter Island." Ana giggled, "Does anyone else see a pattern here? I mean, *Easter* Island?" "So, we're hunting for *Easter* eggs on *Easter* Island?" laughed Hardy. "Maybe we'll find treasure, too!" Pascal added, walking off to explore. Hardy grabbed Pascal's hand, and said, "We have to stay together." They all ran down to the shore and found a pile of scuba gear ready for them–even one for Zeke.

Pascal was thrilled their next Easter egg adventure was underwater. But Ana worried, "I don't want to go under the water! It's dark and scary down there! And something might eat me!" Hardy encouraged her, "The Bible verse from the Easter egg talked about having courage, that God is always with us, especially when we're afraid. What do you think God wants you to do?" Ana meekly answered, "Pray and trust Him." Wearing their scuba gear, Hardy, Pascal and Zeke plunged into the water to see what they would find. Ana didn't want to be left behind, so she waded into the water, praying, "Be strong and courageous. God is with me."

At first, Ana didn't feel much better. But there were many interesting and strange sea creatures. They saw cute turtles, colorful fish, and all kinds of living things, big and small. Ana thought to herself, *Wow! Look at all these amazing animals that God made for me, just because He loves me.* Ana felt comforted.

A strange looking fish swam up, blowing bubbles and urging them to follow. Zeke just wanted to eat it. The fish actually *glowed* and lit their way. The kids followed the light down into the deep.

They spotted an old ship lying on the ocean floor, and swam through a hole in the hull. Hardy pointed toward a glowing door where they'd find the next treasure chest. But Pascal thought, *I bet this is a pirate ship.* He started to swim off in search of pirate treasure, but Hardy grabbed his arm to keep him out of danger.
Together, the group swam into the glowing room and found the next luminous treasure chest.

The next glowing Easter egg revealed two more scrolls!

Back on shore, Hardy said to Ana, "Now, that wasn't so bad, was it?" Ana answered, "Every time I got scared, I prayed. Then I felt better and actually had fun." Pascal interrupted, "What about the new Bible verse and riddle?" Hardy explained the verse, "When you don't listen, it's because you want to do things your way, instead of God's way. That's called rebellion. But God knows what's best for us. God always makes the right

The Bible verse on the first scroll read:

Fools think their own way is right, but the wise listen to advice.

PROVERBS 12:15

The riddle on the second scroll read:

Now north with you,
another land
Where light is scarce,
'cept from His hand
By mountain fire
and glowing sky
On horse's hooves,
you'll need to fly.

choice. Listen to Him." Hardy tried to guess the difficult riddle, "Hmm, up north where it's kind of dark-maybe the Arctic?" Ana added, "Could 'mountain fire' be a volcano? I heard about a volcano in Iceland." Once again, the Easter egg glowed and with bright light surrounding the kids, they were off...

WHOOSH, a cold wind swirled around the kids. This time, they found themselves on a mountain. Suddenly the ground rumbled, and they heard a loud *BOOM*. They turned to see from where the noise came. Pascal shouted, "VOLCANO!" The mountain was spitting red fire into the sky. Lightning streaked in the cloud of smoke above. Red-hot lava oozed out of the top of the mountain, and flowed down the side. And the lava was coming their way! What were they going to do? Zeke yelped and climbed into Hardy's arms.

Suddenly, the kids heard horses neighing and the *clippity-clop* of hooves. Three fuzzy brown horses stomped around, trying to get their attention. Between them was a rickety old rope bridge. It crossed over a deep canyon, and led to the way out. The horses pranced back and forth anxiously, beckoning the kids to cross.

Lava flowed through the canyon below.

The kids stared at the scary bridge, boards hanging by old ropes. Ana gulped. To protect them, Hardy guided Ana and Pascal ahead of himself and said, "You guys go first, and I'll be last. That way I can help you if something happens." "Uh . . ." Ana hesitated, her voice trembling. But then she remembered the Bible verse from the egg, **Be strong and courageous. God was with them.**

Taking Zeke from Hardy, Ana said confidently, "C'mon Zeke. We can do this," and she stepped out in faith. The dog sniffed the bridge, and then hopped on. The bridge creaked, and began to sway. Pascal couldn't wait to rush across. He jumped over one plank without stepping on it, and the boards started to crack. Hardy called to him, "Watch out! Slow down!" but Pascal kept jumping.

With a quick prayer, Hardy carefully stepped onto the bridge. It swayed even more. Hardy hopped gently over a missing plank. *SNAP* went the board he landed on, and Hardy fell! He snagged a rope as he crashed through. Dangling beneath the bridge, Hardy shouted, "HEEEELP!"

Pascal rushed to help, but Hardy yelled, "Pascal, stop! First, tie yourself with the other rope so you don't fall, too." Pascal's first thought was that he could do it on his own. But then he thought of the Bible verse about rebellious people doing things their own way, and wise people listening to others. Pascal did exactly what Hardy told him. Secured with rope, Pascal stretched and reached until he grabbed Hardy's hand. "PULL!" Hardy instructed. Together, Pascal, Ana, and even Zeke, lifted Hardy to safety. "Whew!" breathed Hardy, "Thanks for listening, little cousin." Pascal gave Hardy a big smile. But there was no time to lose; they still had to get to safety.

The kids jumped up on the waiting horses and held tightly to their manes.

Hardy held Zeke closely as the horses raced away from the erupting volcano. *Clippity clop, clippity clop,* up hills and down valleys they rode until the volcano was distant.

The horses came to a lush, green valley surrounded by snow-capped mountains. Another light was shining above them. The kids stared in amazement at the shimmering colors in the sky, even Zeke looked up in wonder. "It's the aurora borealis," whispered Hardy. "I bet if we follow the light, we'll find the next Easter egg," suggested Ana. They traveled along, admiring the beauty, until it was dark.

The horses brought the kids to a glowing house. Hardy jumped off and led the way inside. They found the next treasure chest and Easter egg. The next two scrolls read:

God loved the world so much that He gave His one and only son. Anyone who believes in Him will not die but will have eternal life.

JOHN 3:16

Hardy spoke up, "That Scripture is about God loving us so much that He sent His own son, Jesus, into the world to save us." Pascal asked, "But how did Jesus save us?" Ana answered, "That's a big question. Maybe we'll learn that in the next adventure. What's the next riddle?"

You've done so well, heeded My word. Now come with Me for your reward. He gave His life to bring you grace. Now find the treasure of this race.

Hardy thought out loud, "Well, the Bible verse is about Jesus...the riddle is about being rewarded... and we *have* been on an Easter egg hunt." "Maybe we're going to find the treasure!" Pascal guessed. With that, the egg's light glowed brightly...

A SHINING CROSS stood in a beautiful clearing. All around were luscious plants and flowers in rainbow colors. Friendly animals greeted them. Zeke eyed a nearby lion suspiciously, but the lion rested peacefully with a gentle lamb at its side. The kids felt that no matter what troubles they had, God wanted them to come to the cross. At the foot of the cross was another treasure chest, but it was different than the others. It was radiant, made of gold and jewels, and fit for the finest king. On the outside of the chest was an inscription:

In Him was life and the life was the light of men.
The light shines in the darkness,
and the darkness has not overcome it.

JOHN 1:4-5.

Hardy spoke up, "It's about Jesus." Admiring the chest, Ana added, "This must be the treasure we've been hunting for." Inside was just one scroll that read:

Well done, good and faithful children. You have persevered to the end, and a gift you shall receive. It is the treasure you seek, the greatest of all. Not of this world, the treasure is a light to the nations.

God Loves His children so much. He only wants us to love Him back. God wanted us to know Him, to see Him, hear Him, and touch Him, so He came to be with us through His Son, Jesus Christ. But the world is in darkness, which is sin. Sin is when we disobey God's way and do things our way; and it breaks God's heart. God is holy and perfect, which means He has to punish sin. But God loves us so much He wants us to be with Him. So He gave us a way out of our sin; He gave us a light to see in the darkness. He sent Jesus to take the punishment for our sin and to die on the cross in our place. Jesus takes our sins so we can be forgiven and perfect in God's eyes. That is God's grace, and it is a gift. We can do nothing to earn it. We accept God's gift when we believe in Jesus. Nothing can separate us from the love of God that is in Jesus.

Now go, my beloved children, and let your light shine. Return home to read the joyful message of Easter.

Ana exclaimed, "The greatest treasure of all is—Jesus!" Hardy added, "Now that I think about it, we followed the light everywhere we went today, and it led us to the treasure of Jesus." Pascal thought out loud, "So that's what the light of the eggs means. Let's go read about Easter now!" Then the most brilliant light of all surrounded them.

The kids were back in the attic. They discovered an old trunk with the inscription on the lid:

Your word is a lamp to my feet and a light to my path.

PSALM 119:105

Inside the trunk lay a single item wrapped in velvet cloth—a Bible. Hardy opened to a red satin bookmark and pointed out, "Luke 24. It's about Jesus' resurrection. That's what Easter is all about, how Jesus conquered sin and death and saved us!" The kids excitedly said, "Let's go tell Mom and Dad!"

Later that night, the church lawn was aglow in the light of a cross. In the bushes and up in trees, little Easter eggs glowed brightly waiting to be found. On each little egg was a glowing cross. Eager kids with flashlights ran around searching for the light in the darkness.

Hardy, Ana, and Pascal grinned knowingly at each other. With a bow, Hardy invited Ana to go first. Pascal spotted an egg in the branch of a tree, but couldn't reach it. He turned

to Hardy, and asked for help. Hardy plopped the egg into Pascal's basket. Meanwhile, Ana fearlessly searched the dark bushes for eggs.

Their parents could not believe the change in their children! Hardy was so thoughtful and considerate. How brave Ana was! And little Pascal was actually looking to his older cousins for guidance. "I wonder what brought all this on?" asked Mom. Dad replied, "Let's just be grateful for miracles."

Egglo

ENTERTAINMENT, LLC™

Visit our website for more products, curriculums, resources, ideas, and information

www.eggloentertainment.com